THE TERRIBLE
MR. TWITMEYER

OTHER YEARLING BOOKS YOU WILL ENJOY:

THE TERRIBLE
MR. TWITMEYER

Lilian Moore
& Leone Adelson

Illustrated by Leonard Shortall

A YEARLING BOOK

Published by
Dell Publishing Co., Inc.
1 Dag Hammarskjold Plaza
New York, New York 10017

Yearling ® TM 913705, Dell Publishing Co., Inc.

ISBN 0–440–48734–X

Reprinted by arrangement with Random House, Inc.

Printed in the United States of America

Second Dell Printing—December 1980

CW

THE TERRIBLE
MR. TWITMEYER

1

The Strange Dog Catcher
of West Brook

Wherever there are people there are towns.

Wherever there are towns there are dogs.

And where there are dogs there are dog catchers—like Mr. Twitmeyer.

Mr. Twitmeyer was the dogcatcher for the town of West Brook. It was his job to catch all the dogs in West Brook that no one wanted any more.

He caught sick dogs and took them away.

He caught all the dogs that were left behind when people moved.

He caught dogs that would fight and dogs that would bite and dogs that barked all night, keeping everyone awake.

Every once in a while someone called Mr. Twitmeyer on the telephone to tell him to come quickly and take a dog away.

Then Mr. Twitmeyer got into his little black truck, left his farm way out in the country, and drove fast to West Brook.

When he found the dog he locked it up in the back of his truck—

AND THAT DOG WAS NEVER SEEN AGAIN!

What happened to the dogs that Mr. Twitmeyer took away?

Nobody knew! He never told anyone what he did with them.

That was Mr. Twitmeyer's secret.

And of course the dogs could not tell either. Off they would go, barking and yelping, in the little black truck, never to be seen again.

People wondered. They would ask one another, "What *does* he do with those dogs?" But if they asked Mr. Twitmeyer he would only give them a strange look.

"You want to get rid of 'em, don't you? Well, I get rid of 'em for you." And that's all he would say.

What did that strange look mean?

What terrible things did Mr. Twitmeyer do to the dogs that nobody wanted any more?

People began to be a little afraid of him. When they saw his black truck on the street, they called out to their own dogs.

"Here, Rover, come into the house this minute!"

"Here, Laddie—good dog. Quick, come get your bone!"

Then they locked up their dogs until that terrible Mr. Twitmeyer went away. They really did not need to worry, because Mr. Twitmeyer never took a dog away unless someone asked him to. And you may be very sure that no one asked him to unless there was just nothing else to do.

So Mr. Twitmeyer went on catching dogs and keeping his secret, and maybe to this day no one would have found out what it was if the Noddins hadn't bought a dog.

2
The Dear Little Puppy

One day Mr. and Mrs. Noddin went by the pet store, and in the window they saw a tiny brown puppy. It was a dear little puppy, so soft and round that Mr. and Mrs. Noddin both said at once, "What a nice dog for the children!" and they brought the dog home for Sara and Tom.

Everyone loved the little puppy. She was so soft and so roly-poly and such fun to hold!

"She's just a tiny butterball," said Sara, holding her close.

And that's what everyone called her after that—little butterball.

But just when the Noddins got used to having a sweet, soft, round, roly-poly little dog around the house, Butterball began to grow. She grew and grew.

First Butterball grew bigger than Tom.

"Golly!" said Tom.

Then she grew bigger than Sara.

"Oh, my!" said Sara.

And still she grew. Soon she grew bigger than her doghouse.

"Goodness!" said Mrs. Noddin.

Then she grew almost as big as Mr. Noddin and twice as strong.

Mr. Noddin said nothing. He just looked at Butterball and shook his head.

Sweet! Soft! Round and roly-poly! Where was the dear little puppy that had looked like a butterball? What they had now was a big, rough, noisy dog.

When she ran to say hello to anyone she almost knocked him over. When she jumped up to play with people she frightened them. When she was tied up, she barked so loud and so long that the Noddins were afraid all West Brook would hear her. And they did!

"Butterball indeed!" the neighbors said.

Now it is true that Butterball was big and rough and noisy, but inside she felt just as friendly and playful as when she had been a little puppy. She didn't mean to knock anyone over. She didn't mean to frighten anyone. She just liked people!

And she didn't mean to get into that trouble at the firehouse. It all started because she wanted so much to help.

Butterball loved the firehouse. It was always an exciting place to visit. When the firebell rang, Butterball hardly knew what to do first. She wanted to do everything, to be everywhere, and to help everybody. She ran around and around, barking with excitement. She picked up firemen's boots and hats, and ran from one fireman to another trying to help them dress. Soon Fireman Jones had two right boots and Fireman Brown had two left boots. Fireman Miller had a big hat for his small head, and Fireman Santo had a small hat for his big head. When they all began yelling at Butterball she thought they were saying, "Thanks for helping us," so she would run around even faster, barking even louder.

And of course, when the fire truck went rolling into the street, there was Butterball right at the front wheels to show the way. The driver would shout at her, "Get out of the way!" and Butterball would keep barking back, "This

way, men! This way!" For, after all, how could
they get to a fire without her help?

When at last they did get to the fire, there
was Butterball, right beside the Fire Chief, of
course, helping as hard as she could. For some
reason this always upset the Fire Chief very
much. And one day, when Butterball got so
mixed up in the hose that the water landed full
on the Fire Chief instead of on the fire—WELL!

That was the day the Fire Chief called Mr.
Noddin on the telephone and they had a long
talk. That is, the Fire Chief did the talking. Mr.
Noddin just listened. He moved the telephone as

far away from his ear as he could, but he could still hear the Fire Chief's loud angry voice.

After that, Mr. Noddin took Butterball by the collar, pulled her out to the yard, and tied her up.

"And keep away from the firehouse from now on," the children heard him shout. "You great big—big—pest! If I hear of any more monkey business at the firehouse I'll give you to Mr. Twitmeyer."

Mr. Twitmeyer! The children could not believe their ears. Give Butterball to Mr. Twitmeyer! They threw themselves at their father.

"No, Daddy!" they screamed. "Don't let Mr. Twitmeyer take Butterball! Please! She'll be good! We'll watch her!"

3
Butterball
Gets Another Chance

Butterball seemed to know that the children were worried, so she tried very hard to be good. She stayed near the house every day, and played with Sara and Tom. This made Mr. Noddin very happy.

He was so pleased with Butterball that one evening he thought he would take her for a walk. It was a nice quiet evening, just right for a nice quiet walk. People were sitting outside their houses, enjoying the pleasant air. As they walked past, Mr. Noddin and Butterball would say hello, or stop and visit for a minute. It was just the kind of quiet evening Mr. Noddin enjoyed most after a hard day at work.

But suddenly there was a loud CLANG-CLANG-CLANG! Butterball stood still. Her ears went up at the lovely sound of the fire bell. CLANG-CLANG! Then another sound—DONG-DONG, DONG-DONG! That would be the fire truck. Why, they couldn't have a fire without her! Goodness! She would have to hurry!

So off went Butterball! And off went Mr. Noddin, too! Not that Mr. Noddin liked fires, but he was holding tight to Butterball's strap, and he couldn't help himself. With one hand he held on to his hat, and with the other he held on to Butterball.

People running to watch the fire engine go by, saw Mr. Noddin go flying down the street. They thought the poor man had gone crazy. As he went rushing by, his old friend, Mr. Green, saw him.

"Hey, there, Noddin!" he called out. "Aren't you a little too old to go chasing fire trucks? Ha-ha-ha!"

But poor Mr. Noddin couldn't stop to answer. He had all he could do to hold on to Butterball. And when they got to the fire, he had all he could do to get her away.

It was late that evening when Mr. Noddin and Butterball got home from what had started as a quiet little walk.

"Did you have a nice time, dear?" asked Mrs. Noddin.

At first all Mr. Noddin could say was something that sounded like, "Dang-ding-dang-dang-BLAST!"

When at last he could talk, he told his family just what he thought of Butterball. He ended up by saying, "And this time we've just got to do something about that dog, or we send for Mr. . . ."

"No!" the children screamed. "Not Mr. Twitmeyer, Daddy!" And they began to cry.

"All right, all right!" said Mr. Noddin. "I'm ashamed to walk down Main Street again, or look Bob Green in the face, but I suppose we have to give that fool dog another chance. Only, what's to be done with her? We have to find some way to keep her home."

They all sat and thought. "I know," said Sara. "We can teach her to go fetch things. Then she will be more like a house dog, and she can help us lots."

"All right," said Mr. Noddin. "It's about time she was of some use around here. We'll teach her to bring my slippers to me when I come home, and carry the newspaper in, and things like that."

Everyone was happy about the new idea—Butterball most of all. The family was surprised to see how fast she learned to fetch and carry. Soon she was bringing Mr. Noddin his slippers every evening and carrying in the newspaper every morning. It was fun for Butterball, for each time she brought something she got a pat on the head. She could see how pleased they all were with her new tricks.

Best of all, Mr. Noddin was no longer cross with her. Well, if that was all it took to keep her family happy—just to fetch them things—why, that was easy. She would have to show them what she could do when she really put her mind to it.

4

Butterball
Learns to Fetch

One rainy night, Mr. Noddin came home so wet that he had to change all his clothes before supper.

"It certainly is a terrible night," he said as he sat down to eat. "The rain is coming down in buckets. I thought I'd have to swim the last two blocks. It's good to be home on a night like this. Where's Butterball with my slippers?"

I let her out a little while ago," said Mrs. Noddin. "She'll be back soon for her supper, I guess."

Supper was almost over when the Noddins heard a noise at the front door.

"That must be Butterball," said Sara. "I'll let her in."

Butterball ran through the door right to Mr. Noddin's chair. They could see she was excited about something. Her eyes were shining, her tail was wagging fast, and she was giving sharp, happy little barks. She took Mr. Noddin's coat in her teeth and pulled.

"Oh, what a surprise I have for you," she seemed to say. "Hurry up!"

Running from one to the other, she got the family to follow her to the porch door. Mrs. Noddin turned on the light so they could all see better, and Butterball gave a sharp little bark, as if to say, "There! Just look at that!"

Mrs. Noddin did—and then she let out a scream. There, in the middle of the porch, was a big pile of wet things—big and little things, new and old things, important and not-so-important things, and. . . .

NOT ONE OF THEM BELONGED TO THE NODDINS!

"That's Bobby Heller's baseball glove!" cried Tom.

"And here's Ellen's new doll!" Sara said.

"And Mrs. Hill's umbrella! And I-don't-know-whose shoes and rubbers!" cried Mrs. Noddin. "Oh, dear! Whatever shall we do?"

Well, there really was nothing to do but to

start returning the things Butterball had brought home. Mr. Noddin spent the whole evening tramping back and forth in the wind and rain with the neighbors' things. He was very tired.

Mrs. Noddin spent the whole evening on the telephone telling the neighbors how sorry she was. She was very tired too.

And Butterball! She was not only tired—she was sad. After all, it had been a lot of work carrying all those things from houses up and down the street. And not even to get one tiny pat on the head! Now really! It was too bad.

What Mr. and Mrs. Noddin thought—well! The less said about that the better.

If the children had not cried so hard Mr. Noddin would have called Mr. Twitmeyer then and there. Once again Butterball was given another chance.

5

Butterball Learns to Jump

It was very clear that Butterball could not be left free to visit the firehouse or to take the neighbors' things again. But if they tied her up they must give her something to do. Something that a big, strong, playful dog would like to do. What could it be?

Mr. Noddin thought a long time. Then he went to work.

First he put up a high fence to keep Butterball in the back yard. Then he tied a rope between two poles. On this rope he hung strong rags—some short and some long. Mr. Noddin hoped that when Butterball saw them swinging in the wind she would jump for them.

And that was just what she did. She loved the new game. Not only did she jump for the rags, but she hung on to them with her strong white teeth, swinging back and forth. She liked to see how high she could jump. She liked to see how long she could hang on before she let go. In this way, she had something to keep her busy and happy inside her fence.

Yes, it was a very good idea, but Butterball became a better jumper than Mr. Noddin had planned. For one day she gave a jump that took her over the fence—right into Mrs. Miller's back yard! Perhaps on any other day Butterball might have jumped right back over the fence to go on playing.

But this was washday, and Mrs. Miller had a nice big line full of clean wash hanging in her yard. There were big sheets and towels, shirts and overalls, and all kinds of underwear—pink and white, long and short. How nicely they flapped in the wind!

Ah-h-h-h! thought Butterball.

She tried the sheets first, but Rip!—they weren't very strong. Then the towels. Rip-Zip! Why, they weren't very strong either. Oh, dear! The shirts weren't any better! Now, the long underwear—that was more fun. She got one or two good swings before that, too, went Zip-Rip-Zip!

Mrs. Noddin didn't know that Butterball was visiting her neighbor until she heard Mrs. Miller screaming, "Help! Stop! Stop!"

Mrs. Noddin ran out as fast as she could, just in time to see Butterball make her last jump. It had to be the last jump, for as Butterball came down, so did the whole wash line and all the nice, clean wash.

6

A Sad Day
for the Noddins

The next day Mr. Twitmeyer came for Butterball. It was a sad day indeed for the Noddins, but by now there was nothing else that could be done.

"Mr. Twitmeyer will have to take either us or Butterball," said Mr. Noddin. "The neighbors will see to that."

So Mr. Twitmeyer came for Butterball, dressed as always in heavy boots and thick gloves, carrying his long rope. He was all ready for the big wild dog that he had been told about. But Butterball, friendly as ever and interested in everything, licked his face and jumped right up into the black truck to look around.

"Oh, Butterball, Butterball," Sara cried as

she gave the dog a last hug. Tom put his head against Butterball's coat and whispered, "Good-bye, Butterball, I don't care what you've done. I love you anyway."

Even Mrs. Noddin felt tearful as Mr. Twit-meyer shut the door of his truck in Butterball's face and got ready to drive away.

"Please, Mr. Twitmeyer," she said, "won't you tell us what you are going to do with our dog? We would feel so much better if we knew."

The dog catcher looked down at her and shook his head. "Maybe you would and maybe you wouldn't, ma'am," he said gruffly. And that's all he would say before he drove off.

The unhappy Noddins could only look after the truck and think: Poor, poor Butterball! To have to go with the terrible Mr. Twitmeyer! To go—no one knew where, or to what end. To know only that this strange black truck was taking her where she would never see her family again!

7

Mr. Twitmeyer's Secret

Meanwhile, what was happening to Butterball? She bumped around in the back of the truck for what seemed a very long time. She was beginning to feel tired, when the truck stopped and the back door opened. Mr. Twitmeyer looked in. It was the same Mr. Twitmeyer, and yet it wasn't. Gone were the gloves and the boots and the rope. Gone was the hat over his eyes, and the gruff look on his face. And Mr.

Twitmeyer smiled at Butterball! He even patted her gently!

"Feel a little stiff, don't you?" he asked. "Well, we're safe now—we're far away from West Brook. You can come and sit up front with me."

Butterball jumped into the seat beside Mr. Twitmeyer, and on they went. As they rode, Mr. Twitmeyer talked to Butterball, patting her from time to time. Listening to his kind, friendly voice, Butterball felt happy.

Even if she didn't understand all the words, she knew she was with someone who would not hurt her. Now, that was no surprise to Butterball, but it would have been a great surprise to the people of West Brook. For that was Mr. Twitmeyer's secret. . . .

HE LOVED DOGS AS MUCH AS PEOPLE THOUGHT HE HATED THEM!

He told Butterball all about it. "It's this way," he said. "Lots of people think that it takes a mean man to catch mean, bad dogs. Well, it's not so, but I wouldn't tell 'em that. I just make believe I'm mean so I can keep my dog-catching job. If I keep my job I can be with dogs, and that's what I'd rather do than anything else. As soon as I get a dog away from West Brook we get to be real pals. Just like you and me, Butterball."

Butterball licked his ear, and said, "Woof!"

Mr. Twitmeyer laughed. "I just hope people

don't find out that all I do with their dogs is keep them on my farm. I guess they wouldn't understand that. Wait 'til you get to the farm—you'll find a lot of your old friends there, all having the time of their lives."

The moment Butterball saw Mr. Twitmeyer's farm she loved it. It *was* a fine place for dogs. There was plenty of room to run and play, there were good things to eat, and a good place to sleep.

Best of all, Butterball found that, just as Mr. Twitmeyer had promised, many of her old friends were there, friends she had not seen for a long time.

They were the same, yet not quite the same. What was it that Mr. Twitmeyer did to these dogs that came to his farm? When a new dog came, Mr. Twitmeyer took him out every morning for a long walk and a long talk. He told him things, and he taught him things. That didn't seem like much, but after a while the dogs changed!

Take Sandy—Butterball used to play with Sandy back in West Brook, but she had never liked him. Sandy had been mean. Butterball had never known when he would take her bone away.

And the same with Brownie, who used to live down the street. He had never learned to obey, but now he followed Mr. Twitmeyer around and did whatever he was told. Whatever it was that Mr. Twitmeyer did, it made the dogs feel so good inside that after a while they didn't want to be bad any more.

8

Butterball Gets Homesick

For about a week, Butterball was so busy getting to know the farm, playing with her friends, and taking her walks with Mr. Twitmeyer, that she had no time to think about anything else.

Then, one day, right in the middle of a game with four of her friends, Butterball had a funny feeling. She had to stop playing and sit down. It couldn't be that she was sick, because she had never felt better in her life.

Lady sat down beside her and gave a few sharp barks, as if to say, "What's the matter, Butterball? Have you got a sticker in your ear?"

The other dogs came over too, barking, jumping, and trying to get Butterball to play. She tried—she tried hard, but she wasn't having any fun. She didn't feel sick, but she didn't feel quite right, either. What could the matter be?

She walked over to Mr. Twitmeyer and rubbed against him. Then she gave a sad little yelp, as if she were asking, "What's the matter with me, Mr. Twitmeyer?"

He patted her head gently. "Poor Butterball," he said. "You'll get over it. They all do. The trouble with you is that you want to see Sara

and Tom and the Noddins again. But I'm afraid that's the one thing you can't do."

The only words that Butterball understood were "Sara and Tom," but as soon as she heard them, she knew what her trouble was. She must see her family again! Not that she wanted to leave Mr. Twitmeyer forever. Oh, no! She just wanted to visit the Noddins to see that all was well with them.

Butterball loved Mr. Twitmeyer, and she wouldn't have made trouble for him for anything in the world. The one thing she did not understand was that to keep his job, Mr. Twitmeyer had to keep his secret. And to keep his secret, no dog that he took away from West Brook could ever be seen there again!

Because she did not understand this, Butterball made up her mind to go home for a little visit—just a day or so. As soon as she told that to herself she felt happy again and ran barking the news to her friends.

At first, none of them would believe her. Then a funny thing began to happen. One by one, Sandy and Lady and Brownie and Pooch sat down around Butterball, looking a little sad.

Sandy made an unhappy little noise. Was he thinking of home, too?—of Baby Sue, perhaps, who used to love to pull his tail?

Brownie gave a lonely howl. Maybe he was thinking of Jimmie and the fun they used to have chasing baseballs.

The five dogs gave five deep sighs.

All at once Pooch looked at Lady.

Lady looked at Sandy.

Sandy looked at Brownie.

Then they each gave an excited bark, which said, "Let's. . . . !"

And while Mr. Twitmeyer was busy in the barn, off they went, the five of them, down the long dusty road back to West Brook.

9

Trouble in West Brook

If you had happened to be walking down Main Street late that afternoon, you would have seen a strange sight. Down the street came five dogs—long and short, big and little—one behind the other. You could see they were very tired, for their ears and tails hung down and they were breathing hard. Every once in a while the smallest dog sat down as if to say, "I just can't take another step!" Then the other dogs sat down, too, to wait for her.

On they went until they got to Green-Tree
Street. Turning the corner here, they stopped,
looking about them with tired eyes. Then,
suddenly, barking and yelping, they dashed
across the street. People, frightened, ran to get
out of their way. Someone even yelled, "Watch
out! Wild dogs!"

But of course they were not wild—just very
thirsty. All they wanted was a drink. It had
been a long hot trip from Mr. Twitmeyer's farm,
without any water on the way. And there, right
across the street, was a pretty fountain with lots
of nice cool water spilling into a pool and
sparkling in the sun.

How were they to know that this fountain had

just been put up by the Mayor of West Brook? How were they to know how proud he was of his beautiful new fountain? And how could they know that it stood right outside the window of his office?

Splash! Splash! Splash! How cool! How good!

When the dogs had all they could drink, they jumped in to cool off. When they had cooled off, they stayed in to have fun. In and out they jumped, splashing and running after each other in the water.

People stopped to look, and soon there was quite a crowd around the fountain, many of them yelling at the dogs to make them go away. Suddenly a window opened and the Mayor called out, "What's going on down there? Can't you see I'm trying to work?"

Then he saw the dogs!

Not one dog! Not two dogs—but what seemed to the angry Mayor like dozens of dogs playing in his beautiful new fountain. Bang! Down came the window, and in a minute out came the Mayor himself.

"Get those dogs out of there!" he shouted. Everyone got busy trying to catch the dogs, but the dogs seemed to think it was a lot of fun. After a while it was hard to tell who was wetter—the dogs or the people.

"Get Mr. Twitmeyer!" the Mayor cried, trying to dry himself with his handkerchief. "Some-

body go and telephone Twitmeyer! Whose dogs are they, anyway?"

"I think I know that little dog!" a woman called out. "But Twitmeyer took her away long ago—she was a chicken chaser."

"Nonsense!" yelled the Mayor. "If Twitmeyer took her away, she couldn't be here, could she?"

"But, Mr. Mayor," said a little girl, pulling on the Mayor's coat, "that big dog is Butterball Noddin, and Mr. Twitmeyer took her away, too."

Someone thought the white dog had belonged to the Fuller family. Someone else said he was sure that the brown dog was the one who used to chase cars on his street before the dog catcher took him away. Everybody began talking and shouting at once.

To make matters worse, the fire truck went screaming by and no one could hear what anyone else was saying. At last the Mayor, by shouting the loudest of all, got everyone to listen to him.

"I'm sure you're all making a big mistake," he said. "West Brook has a fine dog catcher. When Mr. Twitmeyer takes a dog away—well, that's the end of *him!*"

The little girl pulled on the Mayor's coat. "That *is* Butterball Noddin, Mr. Mayor," she said again.

The Mayor got very angry. "Go away, little

girl!" he shouted. "Now, then, get those dogs out of there! Where's Twitmeyer? Didn't someone go for Twitmeyer?" He shook his finger at the dogs. "Wait 'til the dog catcher comes!" he cried. "Just you wait!"

10

The Secret Is Out

At that moment all the dogs began to bark at once. They jumped out of the fountain, running to meet a black truck that had just pulled up. Slowly Mr. Twitmeyer got out of the truck.

To everyone's surprise, the dogs did not run away from the dog catcher. No, indeed! Instead, they jumped up and tried to lick his hands and face! They ran around him and rolled at his feet! It was hard to believe, but they were trying to show Mr. Twitmeyer how glad they were to see him.

"Down, Butterball," said Mr. Twitmeyer quietly. "Sit, Lady, Brownie, Pooch, Sandy. Good dogs." And the five excited dogs sat right down again, looking happily at Mr. Twitmeyer.

But if ever a man looked unhappy, it was Mr. Twitmeyer. He looked as if West Brook were the last place in the world he wanted to be. He said a few words to the dogs and they sat down quietly beside the truck while he walked up to the Mayor.

"For goodness' sake!" the Mayor cried. "Twitmeyer—those dogs—they seem to know you! Do you know them?"

The dog catcher looked down at his feet. "Yes, Mr. Mayor," he said in a low voice. "I—I guess so. They—er—they belong to me."

The little girl cried out, "Oooh, they do not! The big one is Butterball Noddin—I know!"

The Mayor stamped his foot. "Will someone *please* take that little girl away!"

"But it's true, sir," said the unhappy Mr. Twitmeyer.

"What's true?" shouted the Mayor. "What do you mean—'it's true'? How did these dogs get here? And what are they doing here—playing in my fountain—I mean, our fountain? Twitmeyer, what *does* all this mean?"

"Mr. Mayor," said Mr. Twitmeyer, "I never thought those dogs would ever be seen in West Brook again. I'm terribly sorry this happened,

but from now on I'll be sure to keep the others locked up on my. . . ."

At that, the Mayor got very excited. He took off his hat and began to fan his face very fast.

"Others!" he cried. "What others are you talking about, Twitmeyer? Talk up, man, talk up!"

"Why," said Mr. Twitmeyer in a low voice, "why, I mean all the other dogs I've taken away from West Brook. I keep them down at my farm, you see."

The Mayor could hardly believe his ears. Whoever heard of a dog catcher who kept a farm full of dogs—dogs that nobody wanted? He came close to Mr. Twitmeyer and looked hard at him.

"Do you mean to tell me," he said, "that we pay you to do away with our bad dogs, and you *keep* them? What for, may I ask? Whatever *for*?"

"I like them," Mr. Twitmeyer told him. "And they're not bad dogs, you know."

"Oh, they're not, eh!" the Mayor cried. "I suppose *good* dogs play in fountains and splash people! And I suppose *good* dogs chase chickens and fire engines! And I suppose. . . ."

In the midst of the Mayor's excitement a car pulled up and a little boy got out and looked around.

"Where is she?" he wanted to know. "Where's my dog?"

11

Mr. Twitmeyer's New Secret

It was Tom Noddin and all the other Noddins. At the sound of Tom's voice Butterball jumped to her feet, wagging her tail as hard as she could. Then, with a WOOF! she rushed to the boy and covered him with kisses. Her happy barks filled the air. It was hard to tell who was more joyful—Butterball or the Noddins.

Soon the family heard the whole story of the runaway dogs.

"Oh, darling Butterball!" cried Sara. "We've missed you so much!"

"Butterball must have missed us too," added Mr. Noddin proudly. "Did you ever hear of a dog coming all this way to get back to her family? We'll never let you go again, Butterball."

"I don't understand this," said the Mayor, puzzled. "If you love that dog so much, why did you tell Twitmeyer to take her away?"

"Well," said Mrs. Noddin, "she got into trouble so much that we got angry one day. It all started because she used to chase the fire truck, and. . . ."

Mr. Twitmeyer went to the big dog and patted her head.

"Don't worry," he said with a smile. "She won't do that any more."

"How do you know that, Twitmeyer?" the Mayor asked. "How can I believe anything you say now?"

Mr. Twitmeyer looked very hurt. "Well," he began, I. . . ."

"Why, he's right!" someone called out. "The fire truck came by here before and that dog didn't even move!"

The dog catcher looked up quickly. A few people nodded. "Yes," they said. "That's true!"

Mr. Twitmeyer was very pleased. So were the Noddins. But the Mayor looked as if he still didn't quite believe it.

"Twitmeyer," he said, "are you sure that Butterball won't chase the fire truck any more?"

"I know she won't," the dog catcher answered. "And what's more, I don't think she will get into any other kind of trouble either."

"That's wonderful!" cried Mrs. Noddin. "We're so glad to have our dog back."

"They weren't all bad dogs," said Mr. Twitmeyer proudly. "Most of them just needed to be trained, that's all."

The woman who knew Lady gave a little sniff. "I suppose you trained Lady not to run after chickens, too, didn't you?" she called out.

"Yes, ma'am," Mr. Twitmeyer told her. "I did! After a couple of weeks on my farm she didn't even look at my chickens. You see," he said, turning to the Mayor, "I've always loved dogs. Seems I understand them, and they understand me."

The Mayor looked thoughtful. "They *did* listen to you, and they did what you told them to. I saw that myself," he said. "But why didn't you ever tell me that you knew how to train dogs?"

For the first time Mr. Twitmeyer laughed. "You didn't ask me," he said. "You just told me to catch them." Everyone laughed along with Mr. Twitmeyer.

"You were good at keeping your secret," said the Mayor. "But now that we know, I'm afraid you can't be a dog catcher for West Brook any more."

Mr. Twitmeyer looked very sad. "That's what I was afraid of," he said.

"No," the Mayor went on, "you can't be our dog catcher any more, Twitmeyer." Then he smiled. "But how would you like a new job? How would you like to be West Brook's new dog trainer?"

Mr. Twitmeyer got red. Then he got white. Then he took off his old hat and looked at it and put it on again—backwards. Then he blew his nose in his old blue handkerchief. At last he spoke.

"Mr. Mayor," he said slowly, "and people of West Brook, I—I just don't know what to say."

"Hurray!" someone cried, and then everyone shouted, "Hurray for Twitmeyer! Hurray for the new dog trainer!"

But Mr. Twitmeyer did not seem to hear them. He was looking hard at his little black truck. He was thinking how fine WEST BROOK DOG TRAINER would look instead of WEST BROOK DOG CATCHER. Now he could call his farm WEST BROOK TRAINING SCHOOL FOR DOGS. Now he could do what he had wanted to do all his life.

AND HE WOULDN'T HAVE TO BE AFRAID THAT PEOPLE WOULD FIND OUT!

Slowly he turned and smiled at all the people watching him. Then he looked at the five dogs

and they began to wag their tails.

"Come here, Butterball," he said. Butterball came trotting over and Mr. Twitmeyer patted her head. "This is all your doing," he said. "If you hadn't become so homesick, I'd still be that terrible Mr. Twitmeyer. You gave away my secret, didn't you?"

"It's just as well," said the Mayor. "But now that old secret is out, I wish you'd tell me one thing."

"Surely, Mr. Mayor," said Mr. Twitmeyer

happily. "Anything you want to know, just ask me."

"Well, it's this," said the Mayor. "How do you get those dogs to do just what you want them to?"

Everyone turned to watch Mr. Twitmeyer as they waited for his answer. How *did* he train those dogs? At last they would find out.

"Well, Mr. Mayor," Mr. Twitmeyer said slowly, "it's like this . . ." Then he began to laugh. "No," he said. "I won't tell you. Suppose we let that be my new secret!"

The MS READ-a-thon needs young readers!

Boys and girls between 6 and 14 can join the MS READ-a-thon and help find a cure for Multiple Sclerosis by reading books. And they get two rewards — the enjoyment of reading, and the great feeling that comes from helping others.

Parents and educators: For complete information call your local MS chapter, or call toll-free (800) 243-6000. Or mail the coupon below.

Kids can help, too!